THIS WALKER BOOK BELONGS TO:

_____

_____

_____

_____

FOR JAMIE EDWARDS

ADVENTURES ARE TO THE ADVENTUROUS

First published 1996
by Walker Books Ltd, 87 Vauxhall Walk
London SE11 5HJ

This edition published 1997

2 4 6 8 10 9 7 5 3 1

This book has been typeset in Stone Print.

Printed in Hong Kong

British Library Cataloguing in Publication Data
A catalogue record for this book
is available from the British Library.

ISBN 0-7445-4792-X

KING ARTHUR
AND THE
KNIGHTS
OF THE ROUND TABLE

PENDRAGON

RETOLD AND ILLUSTRATED BY
MARCIA WILLIAMS

WALKER BOOKS
AND SUBSIDIARIES
LONDON · BOSTON · SYDNEY

KING ARTHUR

Long ago, when forests were still enchanted, a warrior King named Uther Pendragon ruled Britain. When Uther died many imposters, including his stepdaughter Morgan le Fay, tried to claim his throne. So Merlin the Magician decided to use his powers to ensure that Uther's true heir gained the Kingdom.

During the Christmas service, Merlin magicked a great stone with a sword set in it.

After the service all the knights and nobles tried to remove the sword, but none succeeded.

As there were many fine knights who had not attended the service, messengers were sent to summon them.

A tournament was arranged so these knights could try to draw the sword. One such knight was Sir Ector, who came with his sons, Sir Kay and Arthur. It was Sir Kay's first tournament and in his excitement he had forgotten his sword. Arthur offered to return to their lodgings and fetch it, but he found the house locked.

Remembering he'd seen a sword in a churchyard, Arthur decided to borrow it. Without reading the words on the stone, he withdrew the sword easily.

Sir Kay, knowing the significance of the sword, told his father that he had withdrawn it himself, and so must be the rightful King.

Surprised, Sir Ector went to the churchyard where Arthur replaced the sword. Neither Sir Ector nor Sir Kay could pull it out again.

Then, in front of a gathering crowd, Arthur tried. The sword slid smoothly from the stone. The awestruck onlookers fell to their knees.

Then Sir Ector told Arthur that he was really King Uther's son, brought to him sixteen years ago by Merlin to nurture and keep safe.

Although Arthur was only sixteen years old, everyone cheered for him to be King. So in preparation, he was first dubbed a knight.

Then the following week a grand coronation took place and all who stood for justice paid homage to Arthur Pendragon, their rightful King.

EXCALIBUR

King Arthur made his court at Camelot and, aided by Merlin, reigned over a peaceful and prosperous land. Arthur was as brave as any knight, always ready to risk his life for justice.

When King Arthur heard that Sir Pellinore was attacking travellers on the road to Camelot, he hid his identity behind a visor and galloped off.

Arthur challenged Sir Pellinore to give up his sinful ways or stand and fight. Arrogant Sir Pellinore just laughed, charging at his unknown adversary.

The two men struck each other so fiercely that both fell from their horses.

They fought hand to hand, their swords clashing, until Arthur's sword broke.

Knocking Arthur to the ground, Sir Pellinore raised his sword to strike off his head.

But, just in time, Merlin the Magician appeared. He touched the knight's brow, making him fall down in a trance.

As Merlin helped a battered Arthur onto his horse, the King bemoaned the loss of the sword he had drawn from the stone.

Merlin told King Arthur not to worry, as that sword had served its purpose. They were now on their way to fetch a finer sword, called Excalibur, crafted on the mystical Isle of Avalon. The pair rode on until they came to a lake.

Out of the lake rose an arm clothed in white silk and holding aloft the sword Excalibur in a glittering, jewelled scabbard.

Then from the mist drifted the Lady of the Lake. She took Arthur's hand and helped him into a boat which glided, as if enchanted, towards the sword.

As King Arthur grasped the sword, the Lady of the Lake mysteriously vanished. Returning to the bank, Arthur showed Excalibur to Merlin who told him that, although the sword would never break, it was the scabbard he should treasure, for while he had it at his side not a drop of his blood would be shed.

Then Arthur and Merlin went home to Camelot where everyone rejoiced at the safe return of their brave King.

MORGAN LE FAY

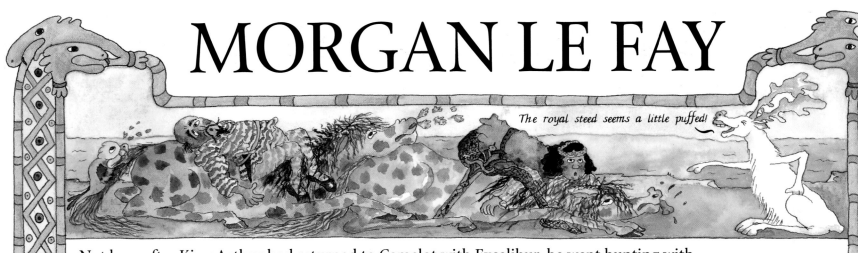

Not long after King Arthur had returned to Camelot with Excalibur, he went hunting with Sir Accolon, a friend of his half-sister, the wicked enchantress Morgan le Fay. They chased after a white hart so fast that their horses collapsed.

While they were wondering how to manage without mounts, King Arthur and Sir Accolon were invited to board a ship moored close by.

Gratefully, the two hunters drank some wine. They were then shown to comfortable beds, where they fell into an exhausted sleep.

But King Arthur awoke in a dungeon. He was offered a sword resembling Excalibur and the chance to fight an unknown knight for his freedom.

Sir Accolon awoke by a well. He was offered Excalibur and the chance to fight an unknown knight in return for Morgan le Fay's hand in marriage.

So King Arthur and Sir Accolon crossed swords, neither recognizing the other.

Arthur might have died had Merlin not appeared and caused the real Excalibur to return to him.

Pulling off his adversary's helmet, Arthur was about to kill him when he recognized Sir Accolon.

Arthur then realized that they had been tricked – Morgan le Fay wished him dead so that she could claim his crown.

Sadly, Arthur made his way to a convent to recover from his wounds. But Morgan le Fay, hearing her plan had failed, followed close behind.

At the convent, Morgan entered the sleeping King's room. Excalibur was in his hand but, seeing the scabbard, Morgan seized it with glee.

When Arthur awoke and realized that his half-sister had his precious scabbard, he mounted a horse and made haste to catch her.

When Morgan saw Arthur draw near, she threw his scabbard into a deep lake.

Then, by her magic, Morgan turned herself into a rock so that Arthur was unable to take revenge.

Arthur returned to Camelot bitter at Morgan's treachery and the loss of the life-protecting scabbard.

Later, a maid brought Arthur a cloak, as a token of Morgan's repentance. When Merlin insisted she try it on first, flames burst forth and she became a heap of smouldering ashes. After this, Morgan le Fay never dared enter Camelot, but everyone knew how vulnerable Arthur was without his scabbard.

GUINEVERE

Look! A beard and long tabard!

OK, ancient one, but not that Guin woman.

King Arthur was growing older. He had long loved the Lady Guinevere and, despite Merlin's doubts, a marriage was arranged.

Mind my table.

It's holding up nicely.

As a wedding gift Guinevere brought to Camelot a magnificent Round Table built to seat fifty knights. Arthur was delighted.

Forty-seven worthy knights took their places at the Round Table and watched as King Arthur and Lady Guinevere were wed.

Is it you, Merlin?

No.

SIR LUCAN

SIR HELEN

When the knights rose to pay homage to their new Queen, letters mysteriously appeared on each knight's seat, spelling out his name.

Arthur hoped to see all the seats filled on his wedding day so, when Sir Pellinore arrived and his name appeared, the King forgave him.

Two seats remained empty. Merlin told Arthur to be patient, for soon one of the seats would be taken by a knight braver than any before him.

Then the words, *Siege Perilous*, appeared on an empty seat. Merlin warned that this seat was reserved for the truest of all knights.

So the Noble Order of the Knights of the Round Table was formed and every Knight swore to fight for truth and justice.

SIR LANCELOT OF THE LAKE

Over the following years many quests were undertaken by King Arthur and the Knights of the Round Table. Once a year, at Whitsun, the Knights would return to Camelot to tell of their adventures and reaffirm their vows. Yet always the two seats remained empty.

One year, on the day before Whitsun, King Arthur was out hunting with a friend.

Before the pair had ridden far they met a wounded knight, carried on a litter. The knight was seeking King Arthur's court, where Merlin predicted that the bravest knight in Britain would heal his wound.

The next day, as each Knight renewed his vow, he laid a hand on the wounded stranger. But none could heal him. Then a trumpet sounded, the great doors opened and in came Merlin, followed by a squire clad in white.

Merlin introduced the young squire as Lancelot of the Lake, so-called because the Lady of the Lake had adopted him. So handsome was this squire that every lady in court lost her heart to him, including the Queen. Queen Guinevere exchanged loving glances with the new knight and Lancelot, looking into her eyes, swore to himself never to serve another lady.

Then Merlin asked King Arthur to make Lancelot a Knight of the Round Table. As Excalibur touched Lancelot's shoulders his name appeared upon the empty, unmarked seat.

Then Merlin placed Sir Lancelot's hand on the wounded knight and miraculously the wound was healed.

King Arthur, who had not yet noticed the attention his Queen was paying Sir Lancelot, was delighted to have one more seat filled. The King was charmed by Lancelot who seemed destined to be a brave and loyal Knight of the Round Table.

SIR LANCELOT'S FIRST QUEST

Sir Lancelot of the Lake was aware that so young a Knight must prove himself worthy. So the day after being knighted, Lancelot set off on his first quest. He rode until he came to a magical town overlooked by a tall tower.

Morgan was jealous.

Elaine made her look like an old witch.

This is an adventure of the highest order.

The townsfolk begged him to rescue Princess Elaine, whom Morgan le Fay, jealous of Elaine's beauty, had trapped within the tower, in a bath of hot water.

It was said that only the bravest knight in Britain could break Morgan's wicked spell. Many had tried and failed, but Lancelot was undaunted.

Things are hotting up!

Fetch me a towel.

Boldly, he mounted the tower. Hot steam swirled about him as he reached the top and opened the door to Princess Elaine's prison.

Stretching out his hand, he led the fair Princess from the scalding water which had held her captive, his brave heart shattering Morgan's witchcraft.

I wish I'd rescued Guinevere!

~ SAVE OUR CHILDREN! SAVE OUR SHEEP!

Scarcely had Princess Elaine thanked Sir Lancelot than the people of the village pleaded for him to deliver them from a terrible fire-breathing dragon, which roamed the land each night stealing their sheep and children.

A princess and a dragon in one day. What luck.

Taking up his sword and shield, Sir Lancelot was led to a rocky tomb where the dragon lived. Using all his strength, he lifted the stone under which the dragon hid.

Out leapt a fiendish serpent as big as a house and spitting fire. Like mad demons the two battled. So fierce was the dragon that Sir Lancelot thought he would be killed. Then, with one mighty blow, Sir Lancelot slew the evil beast.

Stay and recover.

I do feel a little singed.

Everyone cheered their gallant hero and King Pelles, Elaine's father, asked Sir Lancelot to stay with them while he recovered from his adventures. Delighted to be among so many friends and admirers, Lancelot remained there, resting, for many days.

PRINCESS ELAINE

Sweet, sweet Guinevere!

Sweet, sweet Lancelot.

While Sir Lancelot regained his strength at King Pelles' Castle, he thought only of Queen Guinevere. But as each day passed, the fair Princess Elaine fell more and more in love with Lancelot.

Help a poor, love-sick princess.

Oh, magical day!

I'll show you the way.

Say the magic word and I'll give you this drink, sent by your sweet love.

PLEASE.

Desperate to win his love, Elaine asked her father's enchantress, Dame Brisen, to help her.

A ring, resembling Guinevere's, was given to Lancelot, with a message that she was close by.

Making haste to join the Queen, Lancelot was met by Dame Brisen, with a magic potion.

YOU!

I can't help loving you.

Don't leave me.

I am the most unworthy knight.

So not until morning did he realize that it was Elaine, not his Queen, he had held in his arms. Furious, he raised his sword to kill her, but she begged for mercy.

She told Lancelot she was destined to bear his son, Galahad, so he spared Elaine's life. But, maddened by his dishonour, he roamed the land for two years.

He's every inch a Pelles.

He reminds me of dear Lancelot.

I see him in your crown, Pelles.

I just want to be close to Lancelot.

We can't help her, she's love-sick.

Meanwhile, Elaine gave birth to their son, Galahad, who it was said would find the mystical Grail and so save Britain from plague and famine.

Although Elaine loved her son, she pined so for Sir Lancelot that she was soon close to death. Calling her father, she made one last request, which he fulfilled.

Elaine's body was placed in a black barge and set on the river to Camelot. So it was that as Lancelot returned to Camelot he saw Elaine drift towards him. Sadly, he took her body from the barge and buried her close by, so that she would be for ever near him, as was her wish.

It was with a heavy heart that Sir Lancelot took his seat again at the Round Table and recounted his adventures. He feared Queen Guinevere's displeasure but, on seeing the sadness in his eyes, she forgave him, and King Arthur praised his bravery.

SIR GALAHAD

Look at my once fertile kingdom, completely barren, and my people dying in droves. What can I do, Merlin?

Only the magical Grail has the power to cure these ills. Even the great Merlin is powerless.

As the years and adventures passed, Knights were killed or died, but always others came to fill their place. But still the Siege Perilous stood empty. The time came when Britain was devastated by famine and plague which, Merlin told the assembled Knights, only the finding of the Grail could bring to an end.

Suddenly, there was a loud banging as a gust of wind slammed shut all the palace doors.

Then, as if from nowhere, an ancient man, dressed in white, appeared in the great hall.

Then came a young knight dressed in red, without sword or shield.

As the court watched in silent wonder, the old man led the Red Knight to the Siege Perilous. There, golden letters began to appear, spelling out the young Knight's name.

SIR GALAHAD THE HIGH PRINCE

As the Knight took his seat, everyone marvelled that one so young should sit there. But King Arthur was delighted to have his Knights of the Round Table complete at last.

I know it's for you, son.

NEVER SHALL MAN TAKE ME HENCE, BUT ONLY HE BY WHOSE SIDE I OUGHT TO HANG, AND HE SHALL BE THE BEST KNIGHT IN THE WORLD.

Sir Lancelot realized with joy that Sir Galahad was his son, born to Princess Elaine. He led young Sir Galahad to the river where he had, that morning, seen a floating stone with a sword buried in it. As Lancelot had hoped, Sir Galahad withdrew the sword with ease. But still his son had no shield.

Thinking that he could lead them on the Grail Quest, the Knights agreed that Sir Bagdemagus should take Sir Galahad to an abbey where a special shield hung waiting for the worthiest knight. Other knights had tried to remove the shield, but all had come to harm and been forced to return it to the Abbey.

The abbot welcomed the two Knights and let Sir Galahad remove the shield.

Being worthy of the honour, Galahad carried the shield back to Camelot, unchallenged.

A loud cheer rose from the hall as Sir Galahad entered, bearing his new sword and shield.

As Sir Galahad took his seat at the Round Table, a cracking of thunder shook the castle. In the midst of the noise a sunbeam entered the hall.

Held in its light was the mystical Grail, partly covered by a silken cloth. Then, as suddenly as it had come, the vision of the Grail vanished.

King Arthur and his Knights sat in wonder as the Grail faded from sight. Merlin told the court that this was the long-awaited sign that the time had now come for the greatest adventure, the quest for the Grail, which would rescue Britain from the disastrous famine and plague.

SIR LANCELOT'S GRAIL QUEST

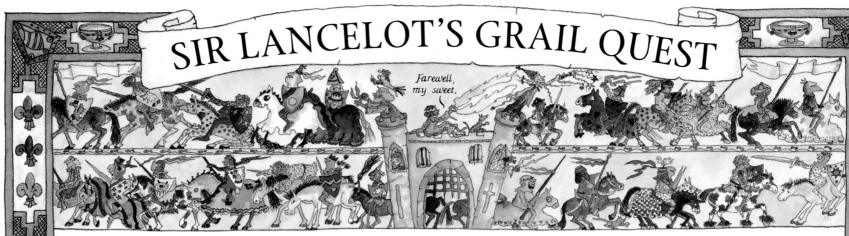

Next morning, the Knights departed in ones and twos to start their search for Grail Castle which had never been found by intent, but where everyone knew King Pelles guarded the Grail. Sir Lancelot and Sir Percival rode out together with high hopes of finding the Grail.

Sir Lancelot and Sir Percival rode without adventure for four days. Then they met Sir Galahad. All three had their visors down.

Failing to recognize each other, they charged into battle. With one swift blow, Galahad unseated both knights, then rode off.

Sir Percival remounted and went to seek news of the Grail from a soothsayer.

Sir Lancelot, angered at being unseated, set off in pursuit of the unknown knight.

As darkness fell, Sir Lancelot lost track of Galahad and decided to shelter in a chapel.

Although lights shone from within, Lancelot could find no way to enter.

Disappointed and cold, he lay down to sleep against a stone cross.

Then, as if in a dream, Sir Lancelot saw a wounded knight approach on a cart.

The donkey stopped in front of the chapel just as the Grail was borne out on a table.

The wounded knight struggled up to touch the Grail and by its power was healed.

The knight gave thanks and the Grail returned to the chapel and the doors closed.

Horses are so unfaithful.

Mounting Sir Lancelot's horse, the knight rode away. Wondering if it had all been a dream, Sir Lancelot tried the chapel door.

The door swung open to reveal the glittering Grail. Sir Lancelot tried to move towards it, but a fierce wall of heat held him back.

Close to fainting from the heat, Lancelot felt himself being lifted up and carried into a castle close by the chapel, where he finally fainted.

For twenty-four days he lay in a feverish stupor. On waking, he realized he was being admonished for the twenty-four years he had loved King Arthur's wife.

WELCOME HOME

A flower returns to this barren land!

Sir Lancelot then knew that although his heart was bold he was not pure enough to get closer to the Grail so, finding the strange castle deserted, he left for Camelot. Once there he received a warm welcome, as few Knights had returned from the quest and many were feared dead.

SIR PERCIVAL'S GRAIL QUEST

When Sir Percival and Sir Lancelot parted, Sir Percival sought out the soothsayer. She told him that the Knight they had fought with was Galahad, and only he knew the magic words which would release the Grail's healing powers. But if Sir Percival was brave he could help Sir Galahad.

On leaving the soothsayer, Sir Percival rode on in search of Sir Galahad but was suddenly attacked by ten armed men. Although Sir Percival defended himself bravely, he was heavily outnumbered. His horse was wounded and he was about to be murdered.

Then out of the forest galloped a red knight, felling men to the left and right. Soon all the men were slain or had fled. Without even acknowledging Sir Percival, the Red Knight spurred on his horse and was soon a fair distance away.

Unable to pursue him on horseback, Sir Percival cried out, sure the Red Knight was Sir Galahad. But the Knight rode on.

Determined, Sir Percival set off after Galahad on foot. Crossing a stream one morning, Sir Percival saw a lion taking a drink.

Suddenly, a giant serpent stole up and twined itself about the lion's neck, half strangling the poor beast.

A vicious fight developed but the snake had a strong hold and the lion was growing weak from lack of air.

As the lion whimpered for help, Sir Percival plunged towards them, slicing off the serpent's head with one deft stroke.

The lion came gratefully up to Sir Percival. Taking his hand gently in its great jaws the lion indicated that Sir Percival should follow him.

For many days they travelled together, the lion protecting Sir Percival from all dangers.

At last, they reached the sea upon which rested a mysterious ship. On the deck stood Sir Galahad and his friend Sir Bors. With a happy smile Sir Percival turned to thank the lion but it was gone. So Sir Percival boarded the ship and the three great Knights sailed off in search of the Grail.

SIR GALAHAD'S GRAIL QUEST

The ship sailed on unguided for four days until it brought Sir Percival, Sir Bors and Sir Galahad to a cove.

There, the three Knights found horses waiting to carry them across the barren land.

Welcome.

By some enchantment, they eventually reached Grail Castle, home of King Pelles, Galahad's grandfather and protector of the precious Grail. King Pelles greeted the Knights warmly, hoping that here at last was the rightful heir to the Grail guardianship.

I'm hungry. Are you hungry?

I'm hungry. Are you hungry?

I'm hungry. Are you hungry?

Are you hungry?

For only with his coming would King Pelles be released from an old and painful wound, by peaceful death, and Britain recover from the plague and famine tormenting the land. As the three Knights were seated in the hall a golden light shone around them.

I never thought I would be brave enough to get here.

Something strange going on here.

What is the Grail? Whom does it serve?

The Grail Maiden entered, carrying the beautiful and powerful Grail from which she served each Knight his favourite food. The Knights stared in awe at the vessel they had travelled so far to find. When the Grail Maiden came to Sir Galahad he asked, "What is the Grail? Whom does it serve?"

Then King Pelles knew that his grandson, Sir Galahad, was pure of heart and rightful heir to the guardianship of the Grail, for only he would know those words. Taking his crown, King Pelles placed it on Galahad's head and so was released from the pain of his wound.

All about them the land became fertile again and the sick recovered their health. For once more the Grail was in the care of safe hands, ready for the time when its healing powers might be needed again and another pure-hearted knight would seek it out.

After King Pelles had been laid to rest, Sir Bors and Sir Percival bid Sir Galahad farewell and set off on their return journey. Before they had reached the bend in the road there was a blinding flash of light as the Grail Castle and all within it vanished from worldly sight, only to be rediscovered in a time of dire need.

So amazed were Sir Bors and Sir Percival by all they had witnessed, that they sought shelter in a nearby monastery.

After a year, Sir Percival, who was an old man, died. Sir Bors decided the time had come to return to Camelot.

CAMELOT

When Sir Bors arrived at Camelot, King Arthur, who had long believed him dead, was overjoyed to see him and hear the adventures of the Grail Quest.
Although King Arthur and his court mourned the loss of Sir Galahad and so many other good Knights, the crowning of a new Grail King and the restoring of Britain's prosperity was the most honourable adventure ever followed by the Knights of the Round Table.

CAMELOT

King Arthur had the story of the Grail Quest written down by scribes for all
to read as it brought great glory to his kingdom. A superb tournament was
held to celebrate the occasion and to honour the greatest of all Knights, Sir Galahad. There were many
adventures still to come for the noble King Arthur Pendragon and the brave Knights of the Round Table
but none of them ever forgot that day.